THE BEST-EVER GOOD-BYE PARTY

Written by **AMY HEST**

Pictures by **DyANNE DiSALVO-RYAN**

MORROW JUNIOR BOOKS

NEW YORK

Printed in the United States of America.

1 2 3 4 5 6 7 8 9 10

Library of Congress Cataloging-in-Publication Data
Hest, Amy.
The best-ever good-bye party.
Summary: Depressed about her best friend's upcoming
move to a new apartment, Jessica tries to cheer herself
up by throwing a going-away party.
[1. Moving, Household—Fiction.   2. Friendship—
Fiction]   I. DiSalvo-Ryan, DyAnne, ill.   II. Title.
PZ7.H4375Th   1989   [E]   88-13208
ISBN 0-688-07325-5
ISBN 0-688-07326-3 (lib. bdg.)

For Sam and Jason
A.H.

To Aunt Gilda who never moved
D.D-R.

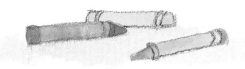

Jason is moving—all the way across town and uptown a bunch of blocks.

"It's not so bad," my mother says. "Some best friends move to other cities, even."

"It's bad enough," I tell her, "bad enough."

Today is the day before the day he goes. Jason's apartment doesn't look right anymore. Everything is cartons, and I mean everything! They are piled neat and high—long, sad, winding rows of them, from one end of the living room to the other.

"These boxes need a number." Jason hands me a purple marker.

"How come?" I say.

"Everything is coded. Number seven, purple," he explains, sounding pretty important, "is the code that means *Jason's stuff from old room to be put in Jason's new, no-sharing room.*"

"Well, I like your old room, Jason."

"So do I." He looks sad but only for a minute. "Although a private room without the twins sounds awfully nice."

"There is nothing wrong with sharing," I say, "nothing wrong at all."

Jason and I take turns printing coded numbers on cartons. Mostly, though, we crawl through box tunnels and cool box caves, and we run relay races up and down skinny passageways. At lunchtime we have peanut butter sandwiches on nearly hard white bread in a carved-out spot near the window.

"The super at the new place says there's a boy on the third floor," says Jason as we eat.

"What kind of boy?" I frown.

Jason shrugs. "All I know is there's a boy. Super says he's just my size. Maybe a pinch taller."

"Well, good for him," I mutter. "Good for him."

Way down at the end of an aisle, Jason's mother is kneeling across a box to tape down the flaps. Jason's mother is not having a good time. The twins keep twirling backward, making little, then big, circles all around the box and shouting, "Cowboy, cowboy!" as they go.

"There is nothing fun about moving," announces Jason's mother between tight lips. "Not one little thing."

"You know," I tell her, "life won't be the same around here without Jason."

"I understand," she says, catching a twin by one suspender. "But don't forget, Jessica, some best friends move to other cities, even."

"That's just what my mother says." I hand her some tape and an orange marker. "I am going home. A person gets tired of packing every single minute."

My mother is in the kitchen as usual. The twins (we have them, too, but we had ours first) are playing freight train underneath the counter.

"Jessie!" They chug toward me and grab at my ankles.

"Tomorrow's the day," I remind my mother. "It looks like Jason gets his own room *and* a boy on three."

"You must feel sad, but don't forget there will be visits. Plenty of visits," she promises, stirring something in a pot. "I'm making spaghetti, Jessica. Your favorite kind with red sauce and chunks of meat."

Jason's favorite, too, I remember.

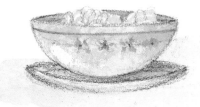

"I suppose Jason's too busy packing to stop by for dinner?" says my mother. "I was thinking...you could make a little party...."

Sometimes my mother has pretty good ideas.

I call Jason. I've already called him three times today, and I hope his father doesn't answer again.

His father answers again. "Hello, Jessica."

"Can Jason come to dinner?" I say.

"I'll send him right up." Jason's father sounds as if this is the best idea he's heard all day.

"Can he stay long, like until midnight?" I say.

"He can stay until eight."

"Midnight would be better. I thought we'd have a sort of good-bye party," I explain. "A person whose best friend is moving away *deserves* a little party."

Jason's father makes a sighing sound. "Jason can stay until nine."

"Is that your final offer?"

"Take it or leave it, Jessica."

I take it.

PRIVATE
PARTY.
NO ONE, AND
ESPECIALLY
NO TWINS,
ALLOWED
BEYOND
THIS LINE.

I'm not sure Jason likes the sign I've made for the bedroom door. "Who feels like celebrating?" is all he says, looking miserable. "What's so great about moving to a whole new place where I don't know a single kid?"

I think about that kid who's a boy and who's a pinch taller than my Jason. "A party's the only thing to cheer us up."

Jason smiles, sticking his tongue through the space where his two top teeth are missing.

"Party props!" I drag a gold-and-pink shopping bag from underneath the bed. We unpack: flashlights and crackers, apple juice in little cans, chocolate sandwich cookies and coconut sandwich cookies, a king-size sheet to make a tent and pillows to make it homey, a book about bears at night and one about the morning star, a pad and two lead pencils—in case we need to send a message.

"Why not *talk* your message," says Jason, "the way we always do?"

"Because, Jason, some things are hard to say."

We make the best tent ever and slide inside with the party props. Jason goes for the cookies right away. Jason loves cookies. "Who licked off the icing?"

"The twins, I guess. They always do."

Jason keeps inspecting more cookies. "I do not eat cookies with licked-off icing," he says in a tone of voice that is not too friendly.

"You used to," I say.

"Well, I don't anymore."

I eat a cookie minus the icing, then another. "Maybe you are getting a little fancy now that you're moving to a swanky new place with your very own room."

"I am not getting fancy!"

I take a coconut sandwich cookie, but the good part is gone. Wait till I get those twins!

Jason flicks on his flashlight. He shines it up and down the tent, then in my face.

"You are wasting the batteries," I say.

"What good's a flashlight if you don't use it?" answers Jason.

"It's *no* good at all if you use up the batteries!"

"Some party," grumbles Jason, leaning forward on his elbows.

"So in your *new* house you can go ahead and make *better* parties," I sneer.

"I sure will," he sneers back.

"You can make tons of parties every single day and every single night!" I shout. "See if I care!"

"Maybe I will!" he shouts back.

"You never know, maybe there are *two* boys in that fancy new place of yours!"

"Or three or four," he says, mean as ever.

I shine my flashlight in his face. "Maybe it's a good thing you're moving, after all."

"You can say that again." Jason lies there, flat on his stomach, mean and miserable.

I am miserable, too, and after a while I say, "I wish you weren't moving, Jason."

"Moving is the pits." He sighs.

"You'll probably have a new best friend in twenty-four hours," I whisper.

"I already have a best friend," he whispers back.

And I smile in the tent. Good old Jason.

"I'm going to write you a message," I say, digging
out pad and pencil. "Try not to read it until tomorrow."

"Can't we *talk* it?" he asks. "Then I get to hear it tonight."

I shake my head. "Some things it's hard to say," I remind
him, writing away.

It takes me a while. By the time it's right, Jason has polished off all the cookies without complaining once. My message is short. It says only one thing, but according to my mother, one little thing can say a whole lot.

There will never be another Jason.

I fold it up and stick it in his pocket for tomorrow.